Brian Wildsmith

What a Tale

Oxford University Press

Oxford   Toronto   Melbourne

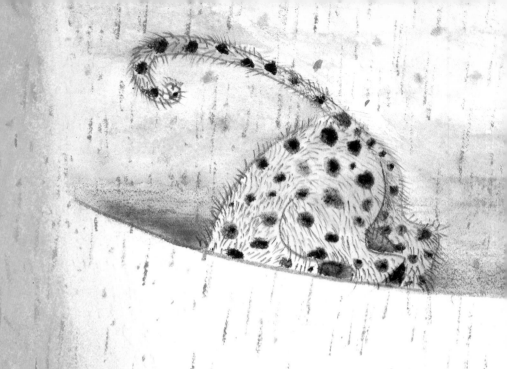

Spotted tail.

Spotted tail, striped tail.

Spotted tail, striped tail,

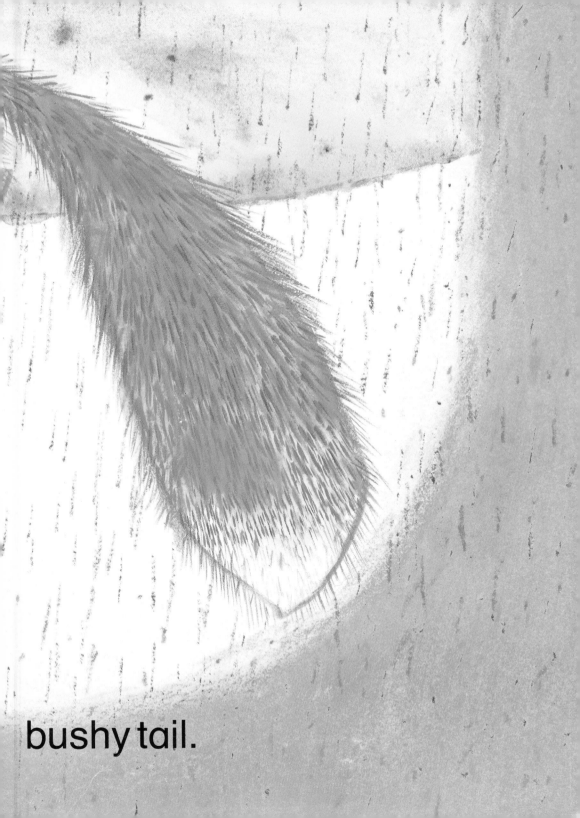

bushy tail.

Spotted tail, striped tail,

bushy tail, bob tail.

Spotted tail, striped tail,

bushy tail, bob tail, long tail.

Dog, cat,

fox, rabbit, monkey.

What a tale.

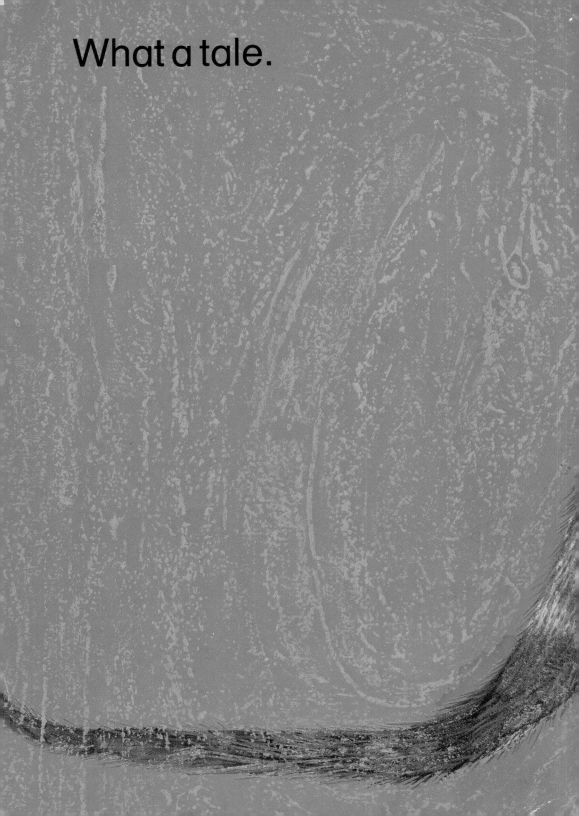

Oxford University Press, Walton Street, Oxford OX2 6DP

*Oxford New York Toronto
Delhi Bombay Calcutta Madras Karachi
Petaling Jaya Singapore Hong Kong Tokyo
Nairobi Dar es Salaam Cape Town
Melbourne Auckland*

and associated companies in
Berlin Ibadan

Oxford is a trade mark of Oxford University Press

© Brian Wildsmith 1986
First published 1986
Reprinted 1987, 1989

British Library Cataloguing in Publication Data

Wildsmith, Brian
What a tale. — (Cat on the mat series)
I. Title   II. Series
823'.914[J]   PZ7
ISBN   0–19–272160–7

Printed in Hong Kong